lettin the

KE

out

evils

BY LOSACK

A BROKEN RIVER BOOKS ORIGINAL

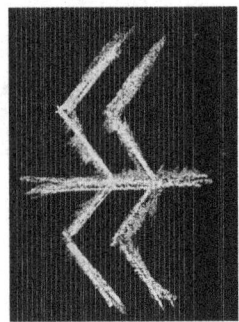

LETTING OUT THE DEVILS
© 2022 Kelby Losack

All rights reserved. No part of this book may be reproduced or transmitted in any form or by any means, electronic or mechanical, including photocopying, recording, or by any information storage and retrieval system, without the written consent of the publisher, except where permitted by law.

This is a work of fiction. All names, characters, places, and incidents are the product of the author's imagination. Where the names of actual celebrities or corporate entities appear, they are used for fictional purposes and do not constitute assertions of fact. Any resemblance to real events or persons, living or dead, is coincidental.

Cover Design by Kelby Losack
Typesetting & Toilet Stall Scribbles by Michael Kazepis

ISBN: 978-0-578-37502-1

Printed in the United States of America

Broken River Books
Norman, Oklahoma

for j david osborne

who the fuck is that

who cares!

ur mom

I tell it like it is, not the way it might be.
Z-Ro, "Devil Ass City"

TRAP BABY

Ari swears he could cut my face off with this shiv he fashioned out of a soup can. Jagged arrow-shaped aluminum with duct tape around the handle, *"m'm! m'm! good!"* scrawled along the sharp tip. He stabs at the glass between us. I tell him lemme see it real quick, nodding down at the money tray for him to slide it through, but he shakes his head, says, "You ain't no killer."

Squints his yellowed glaucoma eyes, pointing at me with the shiv. In a crushed gravel whisper: "You wouldn't even know how to hold it."

Danielle brings a couple 40s to the counter and Ari wraps an arm around her neck, presses the sharp point of the shiv just beneath her vitiligo-spotted eye. She asks for a pack of Newports. Ari sings an old love tune, Sinatra or something, swaying side to side with Danielle in a choke hold. She cracks the slightest smile. Says to Ari, "You're so dumb."

I slide the pack through the tray and scan the beers through the glass. Danielle pays in all coins. She's got that can money.

The schizo vagrant love birds are cracking their 40s and lighting their cigarettes before they make it out the door.

I check the clock on the wall. Last hour of the night shift is always the longest.

Men in fire retardant overalls buy cases of Lone Star and dollar scratch-offs. They try their luck right there at the counter and slide the tickets back for me to toss in the trash.

Some Mexican niggas spill out of a blue candy-painted Charger. They're filming a music video. The camera man follows the rapper inside the store. I pretend to stock the cigarettes to avoid looking at the camera. The rapper mouths the words to the song playing on the phone in his pocket. He throws a rapid succession of sign language at the camera. Grabs a Sprite from one of the coolers. He cheeses real big at the end of a verse so the camera man can zoom in on his diamond grill.

The driver of the Charger dumps coins from a Crown Royal bag, says, "Aye, boss, lemme get however much this is on pump one."

I kill the neon OPEN sign and run through all the closing shit: sweep the linoleum, wipe the sticky syrup off the drink counters, spray the restrooms so the mildew smell is more like synthetic flowers on top of mildew, snake the thick-ass chain through the iron bars over the front door, clip the padlock.

Only lights on the block are the fluorescents over the gas pumps and the blood red moon.

It's a couple-mile walk home with Dillinger Escape Plan in the earbuds.

Rain-slick streets littered with whippets and bright yellow Whataburger wrappers. Dogs barking behind chain-link fences. Reflective orange barrels posted around a long stretch of crushed-up asphalt that will eventually be part of the road again. I stop at the tracks and watch the graffiti'd train cars rattle by, whistle blaring louder than the spastic drumming and warbled distortion in my head.

The flames billowing from the towers at the plant tonight could burn God's retina, but the other side of the tracks is only dimly lit by amber street lamps and the flashing reds and blues of an occasional cop car. In the neighborhood where I live, there's a 24-hour pharmacy that sells cigarettes and a small cemetery behind a used tire shop. A few friends are buried there.

Home is a shotgun house on a lawn that's been uncut for a minute. I hop over the missing porch step and unlock the dead bolt. It's a cave inside. Candle light at the kitchen table where Kira hovers over a canvas, head bobbing to the music in her ears, her back to the door. I slide a hand down the back of her sweatpants and squeeze her butt cheek. She jumps. She punches me in the arm. I wrap her up in a bear hug and bite her ear. She tries not to smile until she can't help it. This is my superpower: being a jackass and getting away with it.

Her kiss tastes like raw honey.

She drops the brush on the floor and I grab her ass and scoop her up in the air. Her fingernails in my scalp, her legs around my waist. I carry her to the bedroom, guided by memory with my eyes closed.

Kira pulls my hair and squeezes my head between her thighs. She bites her lip and moans. Hits that high note.

I kiss her forehead before washing my face in the bathroom sink.

Smell of bleach wafting out of the faucet. I try not to think of brain-eating amoebas.

She's still naked when I walk back in the room. Arms crossed over her head. That playful smirk. I grab the twisted sheet she's lying on top of and pull her to the edge of the bed. Run my tongue in circles over her nipples as she reaches down to unzip my jeans. She grips my cock and pulls me closer.

There's a shrill scream from the other room.

It takes forever to get Emery calmed down. Baby girl is eighteen months old and she wails on and on until the walls of the house fall over, until we turn into skeletons and then into dust.

Kira says, "Poor baby is cutting teeth."

I say, "Again?"

I mean, is she a shark? How many teeth can fit in that little mouth?

Four A.M. Toys scattered across the living room floor. Some violent and colorful late-night anime on TV. Emery walks around hammering on the walls and furniture with a toy horse, singing in high-pitched gibberish.

Kira has her feet in my lap and I'm half-assed massaging them, zoned out, staring at the painting now perched to dry in the window sill. Thick, vertical strokes obscure spiraling patterns of every color. A dripping constellation dots the canvas. The whole thing is more texture than definable shape. Acrylic scar tissue.

"It's something different every time," I say. "Why not pick up a new canvas, call this one good?"

Kira squishes my face between her feet so I puffer-fish my lips. She says, "Did you always look like this? Even as a baby?"

I say, "Yup. Came out the womb with a face full of shitty tattoos."

She sits up and kisses the blue-gray dagger on my cheek. "I'm DJing at 8 Ball tonight."

"You getting paid up front?"

"Drink vouchers and a cut of ticket sales. Steph's boyfriend is performing too. She said I could ride with them."

"Didn't 8 Ball throw a Halloween party with Mike Jones? What, are they broke now?"

"Yeah, they're still bouncing back from that. Nobody went."

I check the time on my phone. Next shift is in four hours. I ask if I can take the car.

"And what," Kira says, "leave me stuck here with this little monster?"

Emery is a growling silhouette stomping her feet in the glow of the TV. It's the part of the anime where the opposing kaiju are now battling each other and the pedestrians of the city below have succumbed to car-crashing hysterics. The giant gator with the lotus flower head drools acid and people melt. Emery bares her new baby teeth and roars. A tank opens fire on the lava dragon. The beast eats it like it's nothing. Emery pounces in her mom's lap and grabs fistfuls of her hair and headbutts her on the nose. The titans rush at each other, trampling over the broken and bloodied bodies of the innocent. Kira lifts the little monster's shirt and blows raspberries on her stomach. Emery kicks her feet and laughs. I'll feel differently when the morning shift comes around, but right now, I'm okay trading sleep for this moment.

Emery is asleep in her car seat. Head lolled to one side, arm wrapped around the neck of a plush sloth she calls Puppy. She's snoring, blowing drool bubbles. Kira tells me to stop glaring at her. I'm too tired to control my expression. Too tired to scream in her adorable face. Lucky little shit.

Preacher Man is already posted on the corner with his megaphone when we pull up to the corner store. Same dirty suit he wears every day. Sun-cracked face dripping sweat. Bible clutched to his chest. He'll be shouting the word of god at cars all day. The word is "repent." Repent and get a gun.

I ask Kira to trade places with me today but she's not going for it. She rubs my chin and says, "Looove yooou." She drops me off at the barred glass doors, the LED window signs flashing lies about how many people have won the lottery here.

"REPENT! REPENT! REPENT AND GET A GUN!"

This nigga I work with, Nasir, he's like the Pakistani Paul Wall, always wearing too-big t-shirts that touch his knees and elbows, neck draped in cubit zirconia chains.

I ask Nasir if his dad's around. His dad owns the place.

"Should be safe," he says, not looking up from his phone. "Old man's got court today. Fighting a DUI."

I crack a Monster from the cooler. "How do you fight a DUI?"

"Old man says he knows people. Bro, check this shit out."

Nasir shows me a video of this kid, maybe five or six, smoking a cigarette and vibing to the new NBA YoungBoy. The kid keeps looking off-camera, watching out for his mom or whoever he stole the cigarette from. Every punchline YoungBoy hits, the kid holds a fist over his mouth and goes *Ooooh*, then continues puffing on the cig and bouncing his shoulders. "This shit fire," the kid says.

Ari and Danielle are outside at the pumps. Danielle is going through the trash bins in search of aluminum cans to crush flat on the ground and deposit in her own swelling trash bag. Ari is popping wheelies in a wheelchair he found who-knows-where, Confederate flag draped across his lap.

It's a slow morning. Nasir and I hang out in the cold storage room behind the cooler doors. He shows me videos of people testing out their 3D printed guns. Some of the brightly-colored Glocks explode on the first shot but Nasir says those are old videos. There's one where a fully automatic rifle shaped like a dragon sends shots right on target without falling apart in the shooter's hands. More pink and blue and yellow pistols. Arcade game controllers firing live ammo. Nasir says some printers only run a couple hundred, and you feed it with this plastic wire like what you'd use to string up a weed wacker.

Need me one of those.

Nasir shows me story reels of hoes he went to school with. Bitches taking ass shots in the mirror between selfies with their kids. "Everybody's somebody's baby, huh?"

The bell over the door chimes. A cooler door opens. Standing there on the other side of the shelves of tall boys is a cousin I haven't seen in some years. I don't recognize the tattoos from his bald head to his fingertips, but the nigga did go to prison and that's kind of what happens, right?

I say, "Raymond."

Raymond leans in to peek over the beers. "Oh, shit," he says. "What up, cuh?"

He joins us inside the cooler. My cousin is not a small person—probably 6'4" and prison buff—but he hops up on a stack of Natty Light boxes and they somehow don't collapse. He cracks the tall boy and holds it out like we're toasting and then he chugs it. I toss him another and grab one for Nasir and myself as well.

"This is Nasir," I say. "This is my cousin Raymond. He was locked up for a minute."

The two nod at each other.

Nasir points at Raymond's forearm, says, "What's that all about?"

Raymond takes his time with the next beer. He sips, wipes foam off his lips, goes *ahhh*. He says, "Dude I bunked with liked to draw these evil-ass clowns, so I had him put a few on me to look scary."

I'm pretty sure Nasir is asking about the swastika and not the clowns, and Raymond knows this too, and Nasir knows we all know, but we go along knowing shit without talking about it.

I tell Raymond I married my girlfriend and we have a daughter now and she's crazy smart, she's our beautiful baby girl, we're just so tired all the time and it's kind of a nightmare but it's mostly pretty great.

Raymond says prison was boring at first, but when they moved him up the state, shit got crazy. He says it can be chill if you stay low key but—and he smiles here, 'cause he knows it—this fool is the opposite of low key. He talks about working the kitchen and trying to get his GED but not being able to stay out of fights. Says they threw him in solitary for a good little minute with his jaw wired shut after some niggas jumped him.

Nasir asks why they jumped him.

You know how a kid will grin like he's trying not to when he knows he's done something wrong, but he just wants the world to move on without acknowledging whatever he did? That's Raymond. A little kid smiling his way out of trouble. I imagine him smiling like that with his jaw wired shut.

"I ain't ever tried to start none with nobody," he says.

The bell chimes. A customer knocks on the bulletproof glass. We kill the beers and move up front.

Raymond says he's been staying at the halfway house up the road, but he's got this friend that can hook him up with a place to crash. "He stay out in the country, though," Raymond says.

I say, "How far out in the country?"

He names a county road that takes me back to pasture parties and drunk driving down suicide curves.

I'm texting all this to Kira while Raymond goes on about the halfway house.

"Bunch of crackheads," he says. "They don't help with dishes, they don't do shit. They come here is what they do—I know you seen them—they pop this fake Adderall shit."

The kid with broccoli hair buying synthetic energy pills puts his hands in his pockets, bounces on his heels.

Raymond smacks the kid on the shoulder. "I'm just kidding," he says, "I'm a big kidder."

Kira texts back: *who's watching Emery?*

I reply: *my mom?*

"It's good they don't do dishes, really. I keep all the knives under my mattress."

Kira: *so she's back on her meds all of a sudden?*

Me: *[blank stare emoji]*

Raymond leans on the counter and nods at the crew of laborers lined up with their junk food lunches. Jeans and trucker hats caked in concrete. He goes on while Nasir rings up the jerky and canned teas. "There's this old nigga who stays there too," he says. "He's pretty cool, but he's crazy, always forgetting where he's at and calling the cops on the rest of us, saying we broke into his house and shit. I told him I'ma stab him next time he calls the cops, but he ain't gonna listen."

Nasir says, "That's crazy, bro."

Kira texts back: *just take her with you... it's not a trap house, right?*

It's the first thing Percy says when we pull up. "My mans really brought his kid to the trap."

We're in swamp land. Out of the green murk grow bell-bottomed cypresses, rows like interlocked fingers choking out a tangerine sunset. A Lexus, a Coupe deVille, and a SLAB'd-out Civic are parked out front of this double-wide on cinder blocks. Extension cords snake through the mud and up a couple trees, plugged in to security cameras. A giant tortoise slow-crawls around Percy's legs.

When Percy was a kid, a trucker dozed off at the wheel and rear-ended him and his mom and he flew threw the windshield and slid head-first across the road, scalped by the asphalt. Where his head was stapled back together is this nasty railroad scar.

He burns down the last of a blunt and flicks the roach. "Been a minute," he says. "Baby girl growing like a weed." To Raymond, he says, "And your ass just keeps getting uglier."

Raymond holds his arms out like Jesus, says, "Don't hate me 'cause I'm sexy."

"Nah, hold up." Percy laughs so hard, he's doubled over coughing. He points at Raymond's forearm, at the swastika. "The fuck is that?"

"Fuck is *this*?" Raymond points at the Japanese symbols on Percy's neck, says, "Nah, nigga, fuck is *that*?"

"It says 'soldier of fortune,'" Percy says. "Because I get money. And I'm a motherfucking soldier."

Raymond sucks air through his teeth, shakes his head. "You got that shit on *purpose?*"

The walls are gutted hip high throughout the double-wide. Pipes and wires spilling out between the studs. We find everyone else in the living room. Bohemian rug over raw plywood subflooring. Leather furniture still wrapped in plastic. A frameless mirror capping off a neon tetra aquarium serves as a coffee table. Hash oil and a three-card tarot spread on the mirror. Asa is in the middle of getting his hair twisted by Briana. She keeps telling him to sit still. One half of his head is fro'd out fork-in-socket-like. He's telling Isaac how he loves to fuck fat bitches. "Hundred pounds a leg," he says, "throw one over each shoulder and—" he bites his bottom lip and humps the air. He jumps up when we enter and it's bear hugs all around.

Emery holds my hand and hides behind my leg.

"She's shot up like a weed," Isaac says. A gold orb fills the empty socket of his right eye and he's shirtless under a fur coat. Skinny torso covered in sigils. Isaac reads tarot and astrology. Been known to get into some shit with blood and fire as well.

Asa says Isaac was just telling him how rich he's gonna be. Raymond asks if Mr. Money Bags is sharing the smoke. Asa sets him up with a glass pipe and a torch and Raymond hits a dab off the mirror.

There's a deer head on a big wire spool in the kitchen where Asa pours up high-balls of Remy. "This the only one you get," he says to me. "Gotta get the princess home safe."

Emery warms up after a little while. She sits on her knees in front of the fish tank, face pressed to the glass, mesmerized by the red and blue tetra.

Briana patiently works on twisting the rest of Asa's hair while he catches us up on his remodeling plans. Says he got this place on the cheap after the last hurricane sunk the property value. "I got the meth heads down the road to tear out all the wet shit," he says. "Probably get them to help with drywall and paint, too. One of them niggas owes me eighty bucks. I'ma tell him, 'look, I'll let you hit a couple dabs or whatever, just come help me knock this out and we straight.'"

There's a series of thuds coming from somewhere down the hall. Everyone but Asa turns to look.

"Hell yeah," Asa says, "I love meth heads. They'll steal your metal, though. That's why I welded a cage around the HVAC."

Raymond leans over to Isaac, says, "Think I'ma crash at your place instead."

Isaac nods.

This scabbed-up skeleton in stained undies runs screaming down the hall. His wrists are duct-taped together. Mouth and ankles red. He bolts out the front door.

Emery jumps in my lap and Briana clutches her chest. Asa rises calmly, pulling a burner from between the cushions. He pops off a couple shots from the doorway.

"Damn," he says. "That tweaker straight Spider-Man jumped over your car. My bad, bro."

The rest of us look around at each other. In unison: "Whose car?"

Asa points at me with the burner, says, "Yours, nigga." And again, he says, "My bad."

Emery squeezes my neck as we head outside to check the damage. Couple holes in the windshield—one low, one high.

"Insurance oughtta take care of it," Asa says. "Just don't tell them you were here."

I say, "About that."

He says, "Damn, for real?"

"Shit's been rough since Kira got laid off."

We stand thinking about how to square this up when Emery rips a wet one. The smell wafts around to everyone within seconds. Hands clasp over faces. So I'm changing baby girl's diaper on the rug and she's entranced by the fish again when Asa comes up with an idea in the shape of a plastic bag full of pink capsules.

"Fuck is this?"

"Supposed to be like the love child of ecstasy and acid. It's got a chemical name, but I call it Kalm with a 'k,' just 'cause."

"Bro, you shot up my windshield. Just give me some money."

"It's re-up season, nigga, not cash flow season. Unless you want to wait a week or so, this is what I got. Shit goes for ten a pill, that's enough to get a new windshield and then some."

Emery walks her fingers across the fish tank. Says, "Fishy."

I stuff the baggie in my pocket and wrap up the dirty diaper and hand it to Asa.

"Guess we're straight, then."

Raymond says he's going to hang out a bit and catch a ride with Isaac. I tell him I'll be seeing him.

I call Kira once we're back on the road. There's the trilling pulse of a trap beat and a choir of hollering drunks on her end.

I ask how the set went.

She slurs, elongating each syllable. "It went grrrreat." She gets quieter, breathes into the phone. "I'm going to ride you so hard tonight."

Just like that, I've forgotten what I was going to say.

"How's it going there?" she says. "How is Emery?"

Baby girl blinks against the wind funneling in through the bullet holes. She giggles. Covers her face with her hands.

I decide to just spill the truth to Kira—be upfront about it—so I tell her, I say, "Everything's great."

DOUBLE SHIFT

I pick up a double to push as much Kalm on the clock as possible. Between the bus stop vagrants and the plant workers, the store is the perfect place to do it, really. It's easy. You ask the customer how their day is going and gauge the direction of the pitch by their answer. Great? I know how to make it better. Same ole, same ole? How bout something to shake up the monotony. One of your day ones got shot in that bullshit down at the beach last night? Here, this will dull the pain for at least a little while. Simple customer service. They say yes or they say no but the niggas who say yes make up for it by copping at least a couple caps. The plant niggas ask if it'll show up on a drug test and I assure them that it won't.

"Nobody even knows what it is."

"So, what does it do?"

"Fuck if I know."

"Lemme get two of them."

Regulars and passers-through come and go, fill their tanks, buy their energy drinks. Marcel shows up for his daily pack of Black & Milds. Gym shorts and cowboy boots and he's already muddy head to toe. Marcel is a plumber and if you ask what he's up to, on any given day, he'll hit you with the same response: "Shit, you know how I do, I just be laying that pipe."

Preacher Man comes in off the corner asking for a cup for water. Supposed to charge him fifty cents but I tell him to grab a bottle. He's out there doing the Lord's work, after all. He says, "God bless." He guzzles a tall bottle of the pH balanced good stuff and then he's back at it.

"REPENT! REPENT! REPENT AND GET A GUN!"

There's this grifter who comes around sometimes trying to sell fake jewelry to people at the pumps. He's always wearing silk shirts and he drives a brand new Audi with his small girls buckled up looking sad in the backseat and what he does is he wears the fugazi shit himself—the fake Rolex, the fake chains, that gaudy-ass pinky ring—and he tells people, "Please," he tells them it's him and his daughters and they're trying to get home but they ran out of money, or he lost his job and they just need enough to eat, or. . . whatever, you know this guy, you've heard it all. And he begs in front of his daughters whose sadness is the only genuine thing about his hustle and sometimes people are dumb enough to go for it. I tell Nasir I don't think those are even his kids but Nasir says they probably are. I'm not sure which possibility is worse.

Things slow down mid-morning. We step outside to soak up some ultraviolet rays, breathe in the ethanol fumes. Nasir hits his Juul pod and looks at his phone. I try out some of the calisthenics he'd shown me on this Youtube channel where these shredded niggas were doing all kinds of pull-ups and shit on whatever kind of sign or iron bar they could find around the city.

I cut my fingers on the bus stop sign. I fall over the back of the bench. I resort to push-ups on the sidewalk.

Danielle has her bag of crushed cans. She's by herself today, no Ari. She says, "I heard you was selling."

I jump up and ask how much she wants.

"None," she says. "And Ari comes around here, you keep that shit away from him."

"Why, what does it do?"

"Makes you see the world how you did as a kid, all innocent and curious. You feel real warm and like your head is floating and shit looks real pretty."

Nasir says, "Sounds like a good time."

"Yeah," Danielle says, "imagine the heartbreak of the comedown."

I promise Danielle I won't sell any to Ari and she limps off to collect more cans.

Ari comes around a little later with a tent rolled up on his back, talking bout how he's been scoping out overpasses to post camp under since he and Danielle were forced from the spot downtown. Talking bout how tough it is sleeping in the elements. Talking bout how they stayed down by the tracks the night before, and how the tent would shake every time a train roared past, and he'd imagine throwing himself under it.

I ask Ari how much he's trying to cop and he empties his pockets. I give him two capsules and wish him well.

Another regular, Martin, he comes in every day for a candy bar and a soda and to vent about the VA riding his ass about his sugar levels.

"I feel fine," he says. "Shit, if Agent Orange didn't kill me, what the fuck is a Diet Coke going to do?"

Nasir and me, we always shake our heads along with him. "Those bitches," we say. "Those hacks."

"First, you get the draft, and you get sleep apnea from firing a tank all day and now you can't even breathe, you know, sometimes you stop breathing in your sleep and so you just don't sleep anymore, and these motherfuckers, they tell you they'll cut off your foot if you don't stop eating sweets." He peels the wrapper on a Snickers bar right there and takes a bite. "Motherfuckers."

We shake our heads. "Motherfuckers."

Martin points at the plastic Maneki-neko on the counter and smiles. He mimics the way the lucky cat waves and says, "That reminds me of my grandson. He just started sitting up. He waves like that. How much you want for it?"

Nasir says, "Oh, that. . . that's for good luck, it's not for sale."

I say to Nasir, "You ain't even Chinese or whatever, give him the toy."

Nasir says, "It's Japanese," and he slides the plastic lucky cat through the money tray.

Martin takes the cat and holds it up like I imagine he holds his grandson to get a good look at him and a tear shimmers in the corner of his eye and he smiles real big and tells us thank you. He and Maneki-neko wave goodbye.

I have an hour between shifts, so I walk home to check on the girls. Along the way, I get passed by a jacked-up truck with a baby doll hanging from the trailer hitch. I don't know what for, but it makes me laugh. Then I come across these two feral mutts pulling a third mutt out of a flooded ditch. I don't so much feel like laughing anymore.

The tub water is green and purple. Emery's been finger painting with her mom. The city put out a notice saying the water is good to go again, but Kira says she boiled it just in case. When baby girl is all clean and toweled off, she shows me her paintings. A dozen masterpieces, I don't know how she does it. I say to Kira, "We made a little prodigy," and Kira says, "I'm jealous of her output."

There's a new painting propped up in the window sill to dry. I say, "Hey, a new one."

"No," Kira says. "Just started over again."

Now I can see it, the layers upon layers of acrylic thick enough to swallow a baby. Colors and shapes buried under colors and shapes buried under colors and shapes buried under colors and shapes.

"Why don't—"

She knows what I'm going to say, so she doesn't let me finish. "It's not done," she says. "I'm trying to express a feeling and it's just not coming out right."

"What is it you're trying to express?"

"If I could explain it," she says, "I wouldn't be painting."

I make it back to the store for the second shift just as Raymond is riding up on a purple bicycle with butterflies in the spokes. No hands, smoking a blunt.

I say, "Don't tell me you stole some little girl's bike."

"I ain't steal it, nigga," he says, "I traded."

I don't ask what he traded for it.

Nasir shows us this article he's reading on his phone about this dude who drilled a hole in his skull to stay high all the time. "Self-trepanation," Nasir reads. "You drill a small hole in your forehead for your third eye to see through."

"This nigga on one," Raymond says.

I say, "How's a hole in your skull supposed to get you high?"

Nasir scrolls for a second. Shrugs. "Something to do with blood circulation, I guess, but bro, check this out." He shows us a picture of a cork screw with a ring of teeth on the bottom.

Raymond holds a fist to his mouth. "That's what he used?"

"First time, yeah. But this is old school. Apparently, it's the oldest operation in the world."

"I'd have heard of that by now," Raymond says. "I call bullshit."

Kira gets called for an interview, so she drops Emery off at the store for a bit.

"You're sure it's fine?" she says.

I say, "Yeah, it'll be great. She can help me stock the beer cooler."

Nasir lifts Emery onto the counter and baby girl squishes her face against the bulletproof glass and laughs.

I give Kira a kiss. Tell her good luck and not to worry.

"He's got plenty of help here," Raymond says as he contemplates which bag of chips to steal.

Kira says, "If it's too much, call me."

I tell her it won't be. I give her another kiss.

Kira rubs her nose against Emery's behind the glass. Says, "I love you, baby girl."

Emery says, "Bye bye, momma."

Kira blows one last kiss from the car with the duct-taped Xs over the bullet holes.

Raymond goes for the bag of spicy Doritos. He's got this big grin on his face.

I say, "What?"

He says, "You're so soft around your family."

I say, "Duh, nigga."

I scoop Emery off the counter and airplane her over to the knife cabinet where all the bongs and brass knuckles are locked up and I ask her what she wants for Christmas.

The boss shows up to grab a few hundred bucks from the register and dip. He's placing a bet on the game. "You don't even know which game, do you?" he says to Nasir.

Nasir says, "No, Dad. No clue."

Khan pinches his son's cheek, says, "That's why you're going places. Too good for silly things like sports."

Khan points down at Emery shuffling the cigarillo packets out of order, counting and naming the colors as she does so.

"Fuck is this, we a daycare now?"

I say, "New hire. I'll train her right, boss."

He kneels down and says to Emery, "Whatever these clowns tell you, do the opposite. Okay? That's some life advice for you, kiddo."

Emery pouts her lips. Starts crying. She runs over for me to pick her up.

Khan says, "What? What'd I do?"

I shake my head. "You're good," I say. "She probably just thinks you're ugly."

Raymond draws a hop scotch grid on the sidewalk. He's showing Emery how it's done when Mr. Fugazi rolls up and puts one of his fake chains on baby girl's neck. "For the princess," he says. Raymond taps on the window and shouts, "Need a twenty. Baby girl wants a chain." I roll my eyes. I take the cash from the register.

I wish I could climb inside the camera above the cash box and fast forward the rest of the shift. Changing diapers on the counter. Mopping the vomit of a drunk who stumbles in off the bus. Ringing up customers while Emery throws a tantrum on the floor. Calming baby girl down with a milk carton and a tuner car magazine. Telling Ari to fuck off when he comes around begging for more Kalm and I have to tell him there is no more, it's sold out, which is only a couple capsules away from being a lie. Nasir endlessly scrolling his phone. Raymond pushing how many beers I'll let him steal, knowing I don't buy the whole "put it on my tab" bit. Kira rolling up to take Emery home, saying they want her back for a follow-up interview, shrugging her shoulders when I ask who this was again talking about hiring her? Fuck it, it's a job, I guess. Hope for her sake, it's better than this one.

I hide in the coolers and build a bed out of beer boxes. As soon as head hits balled-up hoodie, I'm out, off to the concrete world again. It's always the same in my dreams—a warehouse, an aqueduct, a stairwell—always somewhere concrete and vacant. Industrial emptiness. Nothing ever happens in the concrete world. Even the pack of eyeless feral dogs are empty threats, always lurking, never attacking. They stand as tall as freight trucks, these monstrous dogs—some kind of hound breed—malnourished and baring teeth. But they don't do shit. It's me and the dogs, going nowhere, doing nothing.

Nasir is going on again about the people with holes in their heads. This time, it's about a woman, Amanda Fielding, claiming trepanation is not only the path to higher consciousness, but a remedy for mental illness. She'd know, I guess, 'cause in the '70s, Amanda drilled a hole in her own head when she couldn't find a doctor to do it for her.

Nigerian kids in the '60s, the Hindu god Shiva, niggas ten thousand years ago were cutting out chunks of their skulls to achieve higher consciousness. Up until lobotomies became the hype, doctors would trepan patients to relieve migraines and epilepsy. The esoteric explanation is that a hole in the third eye chakra is like a window to let the devils out.

Raymond says, "Shit, that's what I need."

"Hell no," Nasir says. "In case I get in a tussle, I don't need an off switch."

Preacher Man has gone hoarse from all the shouting to repent, to repent and get a gun. His voice is soft and scratchy even over the megaphone. Words won't do it anymore. He has to lead by example. So he sets the megaphone on the ground and crosses his arms inside his jacket. Takes out a Bible in one hand, Desert Eagle in the other. He raises both in the air. At least a couple niggas must have heard his message. They rush him on either side and put one in his dome and a few more in his back. Raymond decides to dip before the cops show up.

There's an emptiness to the place even though it gets busier as the night goes on. I sell out of Kalm. Nasir says he's got a thing with this girl and I tell him it's all good, I'll close up. So it's just me and the vagrants and the loud-mouthed teenagers. The barefoot nigga changing his oil right there in the parking lot. The EMTs with their midnight coffees. The schizos dancing up and down the aisles, painting feces on the restroom walls. Feel like we all could use a drill to the skull.

I go through all the closing shit. The toilets, the trash, the money. I'm clipping the padlock around the chain on the front door when Ari walks up muttering to himself the way he does and sinks that soup can shiv in my side, the jagged aluminum scraping against my hip. He digs it in there by sandwiching me up against the wall and I might be helping the way I fall back against him to shove him off. Ari stumbles back a couple steps and I punch him in the eye. He trips over a parking curb. Falls on his back. I pull the shiv out of my side and I ain't gonna lie, I might cry a little bit, but the shit being all jagged makes it hurt more coming out. Ari staggers to his feet. Slurring from biting his tongue, he says, "You made me remember," and he rushes me, head down like a bull. Pins me against the ice machines. I drop some elbow shots on his back and throw a knee to his chin and this time when he goes down, I go down with him and keep swinging on his bitch ass.

CUTTING
CUTTING
CUTTING
TEETH
TEETH
TEETH

Emery's face is contorted in a scream. She's been going at it for so long, though, all I hear is this steady high-pitched ringing. Bubbles and bath water drip from my chin. Emery's face has gone red, streaked with tears. Baby girl is cutting another tooth.

Again this morning, I'm checking stitches in the mirror, never sure if the heat is some natural part of the healing process or blood spilling from a thread come unraveled. Asa calls and Emery's still screaming and I tell him that it's cool, to just ignore it, and he says he's got a favor to ask. Says he'll make it worth my time but he's wondering if I can hit the Kalm re-up in his place.

"Gotta take Donatello to the vet," he says. "Nigga been acting all lethargic, moping about."

I say, "The tortoise?"

Kira is at her follow-up interview. It's me and the kid and I am not taking Emery to the re-up, so when Raymond sends picture #5 from his used car lot tour, I'm not even looking at it but I text back, *that's the one. Get it and scoop me from mom's.*

Emery and I ride the bus to my mom's. On the bench across from where we sit is a man with his legs stretched way out. His clothes have holes all over them and he smells like shit and he's obviously rolling. This old lady with a walker shouts at him to move. She runs over his feet and takes a seat right next to him. The man doesn't move, save for his head lolling over to one side, and he says, "Lady, you just sealed your fate."

The lady stares daggers into the man's eyes. Says, "I told you to move."

My mom's apartment is a time capsule. There's pictures of five-year-old me and there's the TV with copper and light bulbs in its guts and there's non-perishables in the pantry that have probably definitely perished by this point. I tell her I won't be long. I promise to not be long. She tells me not to worry, she's already bouncing Emery on her knee and enjoying being a grandma and I hate we don't do this on the regular, but there's a clusterfuck of pill bottles on the kitchen table that she'll never explain to me in a way that lets me help her and I ask one more time if she's sure about this and she says if I don't leave, she'll throw my ass out and so I kiss them both on the forehead and I go.

I didn't mean to encourage Raymond to get a PT Cruiser. I tell him when this is over, he should take it back, before the ink dries on the contract.

"No worries," he says, "this is the test drive." He lifts the brim of his Rockets hat to show the bandage wrapped around his head. Dry blood spot over his third eye.

I say, "You really fucking did it."

"I feel the exact same," he says, "but better. Not bogged down by bullshit, you know. Just riding the wave. It really is like letting out the devils."

"I'll take your word for it."

"I've decided I'm not going to cover this," he says, flashing the swastika on his forearm. "You can't erase history. All you can do is own it and figure out where to go next."

"Well, you're a charmer," I say. "And good in a scrap, if the charm doesn't work. You'll be fine, I guess."

He says he's been getting in fights on social media. Says, "This thing is bad for me," holding up his phone.

I say, "Yeah, you were probably better off not having one."

"Nah, I had one on the inside."

"The fuck?" I say. "How?"

"Nigga, it's the same world in there as it is out here," Raymond says, "just a boxed-in version of it."

Donatello the tortoise pokes his head out of the rear passenger window of Asa's Coupe deVille. Asa loads a duffle bag full of cash in the trunk of the PT Cruiser. First, he has each of us feel the weight of it. Says, "You should be getting a bag from my guy that weighs about the same, but it'll be full of Kalm." He goes on: "You'll find him at the jetties. Korean nigga. He'll be fishing."

Raymond says, "Should we be strapped?"

Asa says, "Are you not always?"

"I just got out the joint, fool."

"Yeah," I say. "I ain't got a gun on me, either."

"That is shameful," Asa says. "Ain't you a family man?"

"My shit's down at the pawn shop. Times have been tough."

Asa says, "Hold on a minute," and he heads inside the trailer and when he comes back out, he's carrying an I-don't-know-what, but it's got a pistol grip with a long barrel and a banana clip. He hands it to me and says, "Probably won't fit in your waist band, but you up this bitch on any nigga, he not gonna know what the fuck to do besides pray."

"Draco?" Raymond says.

"Kel-Tec. PLR. This a .40, shorty."

I up it with one hand, aim at a tree.

Asa says, "Go ahead."

I squeeze the trigger and imagine how the inside of a tank must sound when it fires. The kick knocks me back a couple steps.

Asa laughs. "Tony Montana gun right there, boy."

Donatello's head shrinks back inside the car and the window rolls up.

We creep through the lot bumping Z-Ro, getting amped up, looking out for anyone who might be looking out for us. *"I ain't a killer but please don't push me, baby. . ."*

It's crazy packed down at the jetties. Damn near every rock is occupied by someone fishing or just vibing to the sounds of the ocean. The blend of hair metal and sad country and clicka in the air. We walk to the end where the waves crash over the pavement and then we walk back.

"I think that's him," Raymond says.

We climb down the rocks to sit on either side of this big Asian dude in a Rockets jersey. He unhooks a kingfish and drops it in the cooler with a few others. The man says hello. He casts another line out. I tell him Asa sent us. He says, "Who?"

A rock flies through the air and nicks Raymond's ear and he hisses. Hand to the side of his head. The old man who threw the rock glares silently in our direction.

"No," I say to Raymond, "pretty sure that's him."

The old man stays silent for a while. We're taking in the sounds of the waves and the gulls, the barges coming in to dock. The smell of fish guts and salt. After a while of nothing biting his line, the old man says, "You were told to look for the Korean fisherman."

I say, "Yeah. You him?"

"I am. That man you sat next to over there is Filipino."

"That's my bad, dawg," Raymond says, quickly adding, "Sir."

"How you want to do this?" I say.

"You have the money, yes?"

"Yup."

"The product is at the bottom of my ice chest."

Both of us reach to open the chest at the same time. Inside is a baby bull shark, thrashing and biting the air. The man has stopped watching the line to turn and see what we'll do. Raymond and I share a look. We can't be bitch-made in front of the supplier. We reach inside the ice chest and the man doubles over trembling, trying to hide his laughter.

"You fucking morons," he says. He stands and closes the lid of the ice chest. Then he says, "Follow me."

We do the trade-off in the parking lot. Bag of this for a bag of that.

The old man being further up the distribution chain, I figure I'll ask him where this shit comes from, originally.

He shrugs. "Fuck if I know," he says. "I'm just a fisherman."

We drop the shit back at Asa's and he gives each of us a couple hundos.

Raymond says, "How's the turtle? Is he gonna make it?"

"Oh, yeah," Asa says, "this nigga's got five hundred more years in him, easy. Doc said he just needs more exercise. He's got it too good. Spoiled brat."

Donatello crawls around the yard, slow as hell.

I offer the burner back to Asa but he holds a hand up, shakes his head. "Hold on to it," he says. "You a family man, can't get caught lacking."

Mom's apartment is littered with toys from my childhood and she hasn't answered my phone calls and there's a quiet to the place that makes me sick to my stomach from the moment I walk in shouting *mom? MOM?!* and I can't remember if that pill bottle was toppled over like that when I left and I run down the hall, *EMERY! MOM!*, and find them both in the bedroom, my mom asleep, Emery playing with the novelty Avon perfume bottles on her vanity. I scoop Emery up in my arms and press my face against hers and say I love her so much and my mom—I have to shake her awake—I tell her thank you and admit I was a little worried leaving Emery with her for so long. My mom rolls her eyes into focus, pops her jaw. She smacks me on the shoulder and says, "Raised you, didn't I? You turned out decent, I guess."

Kira squeezes tubes of emerald and gold over a dried layer of salamander and cyan, smearing the new colors all over the canvas, covering the old, creating and masking her own history. The interview was a bust. She says everyone she'd met before from the company showed up with their heads shaved. And there were people she hadn't met before and they also had shaved heads. And everyone was wearing grey robes. "It was a fucking cult," she says. "I should have known. What kind of job interview takes place at a beach house." She's got paint up to her elbows, in her hair, across her face. Spattered all over the table and floor, all over my shirt when I pull her in close to promise her we'll be alright. We're gonna make it.

"Dinosaur"

Khan hits me up after a couple days, wants to know why I haven't been showing up to work. I remind him I was stabbed and he tells me not to worry about coming in anymore, so that's that. I go to the bank to see about getting a personal loan. I've had enough time icing the stitches to do the math. If I can go in with Asa on a bigger re-up, say a thousand capsules, we might could talk the price down to half. Bulk deal. Then we spend a week driving around Texas, hitting truck stops and concerts and sleeping in the car. Should double the front cost easy. Tax the shit the further we drive to cover gas. Then it's fuck a job, for me and Kira both.

"What do you plan on using this loan for?"

I'm thinking of how to answer when Spider-Man and a Luchador come in waving guns around. A .22 pistol and the type of shotgun you crack over your knee to reload. These gotta be some kids. But they wave the guns they stole from their parents and they shout at everyone to get on the ground, so that's what everyone does. I've got my hands behind my head lying face down just waiting for it all to be over, going over the math again in my head, hoping I got this figured out right, that I'm not just tripping.

After the bank is done getting robbed and the kids run away, the bankers are busy talking to the cops who show up two minutes too late. I tell the lady at the front I'll be back when things are less hectic.

Kira sends me a nude. A mirror selfie. She's covering her tits with her arm, being a tease. The text reads, *bout to get in the shower. . . how much longer will you be?*

I take all the shortcuts home, cutting through parking lots at red lights. The shower is still running when I burst through the door. I strip on my way to the bathroom and almost slip getting into the tub and off top, we start going at it.

I trace the water droplets on her neck with my tongue. She hooks a leg around my thighs and I lift her up, press her against the wall, knocking the ABCs off the tile. I slide in slow at first and she flexes her pussy around my dick like she's trying to choke it and I go in harder and she digs her fingernails in my back.

I'm seconds away from climax when the door flies open.

The little voice outside the curtain says, "I go potty!"

Sabotaged once again. I hang my head as Kira reaches around the curtain to lift Emery onto the toilet and hold her there so she doesn't fall in. "You're such a big girl," she says. "Look at you."

I crank the temperature all the way to cold.

We go for a walk around the neighborhood. Trunk-rattling bass transitions to tejano and then to pop country and back again to the bass. There's a group of kids fishing for crawdads in the drainage ditch. Front lawn barbecues. Camo-clad legs hanging out the hood of a gutted truck. An old woman braiding hair on her front porch.

A little boy with a mouth full of silver follows us on his bike.

Kira nudges Emery.

"Say hi."

Emery wraps her arm around my leg.

The boy says, "Maybe she wants me to do a trick."

I say, "Go for it."

He says, "I don't know any tricks."

We walk on.

Kira says, "I think I've gone too far with the painting. It's past saving. I'm just going to start over."

"It looks cool, though. You could sell it and start on another canvas."

"Nah, I'm not feeling it. I'll probably drown it in lacquer and start all over."

There's a giant deflated alligator gar at the mouth of a storm drain. Belly up, throat slit.

Emery jumps up and down, tugging on the hem of my shirt. She says, "Dinosaur!"

Back home, Emery brings me books to read. Dancing gorillas and hungry caterpillars and insects that speak gibberish.

Kira scrolls her phone. "What time were you at the bank this morning?"

"Oh, yeah," I say, "that bitch got robbed."

"By sophomores, apparently. One of them snitched. They both got picked up in class."

"They went back to school after hitting the bank?"

"I mean, it'd make a good alibi, if one of them wasn't a snitch."

I kiss Emery on top of the head and squeeze her to my chest. I tell her, "Be picky who you're friends with."

Kira gives her a big smooch on the cheek, says, "That's right, baby girl. No snitches."

Emery smacks us both in the head with the gorilla book and roars. She holds her hands up like claws and says, "Dinosaur!"

new kind of Bullshit

I need some right-now money to keep the phones on, so I hit up Percy.

"Yeah, I've got some work," he says. "But come prepared for some bullshit."

The bullshit is running new duct work in this cramped attic. We're hunched over like the second monkey on the evolution chart, tightrope-walking along the studs. There's fresh insulation, too, that fluffy spray type that gets all over your clothes and in your hair. The fiberglass sets my arms on fire, but it's money. Can't complain.

I'm dragging these long robot arms from the unit to the vents and I tell Percy thanks again, I really needed this, and then something hisses in the dark. Percy shines the flashlight around and spots this coon standing on its hind legs. Snarling. I slip off the two-by-four and fall through the ceiling. I land on my back on the kitchen table. That fresh, fluffy insulation and little pebbles of broken drywall rain down from the me-sized hole in the ceiling. I tell the toddler and his grandmother who just sat down for Spaghetti-O's, I tell them, "My bad."

old devils

I'm eight years old, so Raymond's gotta be five, maybe six—it's the summer he has a gap between every couple of teeth, all the babies falling out—and we're in the abandoned church where the older kids make out and huff paint. It's a small church, nothing but a sanctuary with four graffiti-covered walls and a caved-in ceiling.

Raymond stands behind the knife-tagged pulpit. On the wall behind him is a giant pentagram and the word 'bitches' tagged in neon pink. He screams John 3:16 at the empty room, karate chopping the air on emphasized words. *God. . . begotten. . . perish*.

I run across one dusty pew and jump to another. I throw a hymnal through what's left of a stained glass window. Blue and yellow shards catch sunlight. I piss in a corner.

I'm eight years old. I mean nothing by it.

Raymond screams about eternal life.

I don't know why I went back this far, why I'm telling you this, but maybe it's just 'cause like, I was thinking about Raymond, how he would preach the gospel in this dilapidated church when we were kids, and also how he used to tear up strips of construction paper and eat them and swear the different colors had their own flavors, and now we're both grown and he's done time for cutting some nigga's face open with a beer bottle and I have a kid of my own.

It's wild to think about.

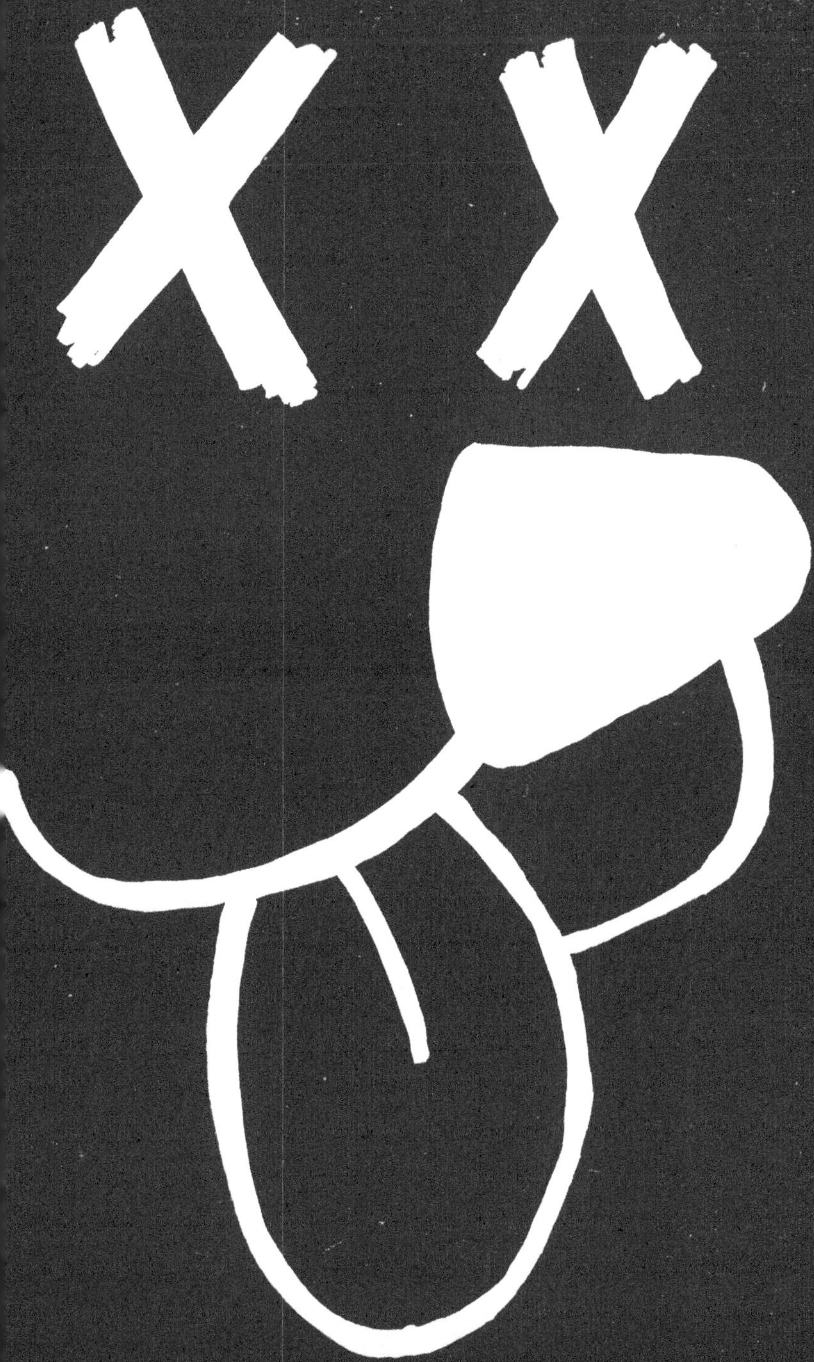

Raymond is out on the stoop bottle-feeding a goat when I pull up to Isaac's. A modest adobe on a couple acres of crunchy yellow grass. The Frankenstein towers of a power plant looming in the background. White noise of electric humming. A few chickens peck around the yard. One flaps down from the hood of Isaac's green candy-painted/gold wire-wheeled Civic.

I've come here because I want to try the Kalm, and I need a safe place to trip. I need something to smooth out the manic waves in my head, take me outside of myself for a bit.

Raymond says I won't need any drugs if I drill a hole in my head like he did. Or holes, more like. An ellipses of raw meat dots his forehead. He touches the freshest of the scars, says, "This is the one. This time, it'll last."

Isaac, though, I tell him and he asks how much I brought and I show him the two capsules and he says, "Let's fix you up right," and he breaks the capsules open and sprinkles the powder into a pot of boiling milk and when it's stirred and changed colors, he pours up a glass and says, "Drink it. But sit down first."

In the den is a gold-trimmed couch with cherub pattern upholstery, something you'd see in a castle. A portrait of Amy Winehouse hangs on the wall and there's a shrine to Santa Muerte over in the corner.

Isaac separates the lids of his right eye and slides a milky white pearl inside the cavity. Blinks a few times. He's dressed to the nines. Paisley blazer/wingtip gaiters/neck weighted down with chains.

"Got some business to see to," he says on his way out the door, shadow stretched tall across the carpet by the light of the afternoon sun. "Good luck on your journey."

Raymond joins me on the cherub couch. He's still cradling the goat.

"Are its legs broken?" I say.

Raymond says, "Nah, she's just going through this phase where she don't want to be put down. You know how it is."

The goat bleats.

At some point, the Kalm hits, and everything takes on a low-res, sharp polygonal quality. Colors turn dull and grungy. Raymond and the goat are still here with me on the couch, but now they look like their skeletons are made of bricks. Think PS1 graphics.

Raymond says, "The shit hit, huh? How's it feel?"

I can't remember how to talk, so I smile and nod. I get up and walk around the room for a bit, getting a feel for the controls. I open up the front door and a load screen appears. Three feral dogs—lights beaming from hollow eye sockets—sprint across a pitch black horizon. When the world comes back into focus, I'm suddenly at the jetties, watching pixels dance across the waves. It's peaceful until the giant feral dogs across the water go stomping through the chemical plant, making shit explode. My first thought is I have to find the girls and we have to escape before the city becomes one big crater in the earth. I hop in my car, but I can't drive so well—basic motor skills gone fuzzy the way they do in dreams—so I'm cutting down palm trees and traffic lights and screaming pedestrians until finally, I flip the bitch over the bridge, bailing as the car somersaults through the air, and when I face-plant in the muddy bank, my health bar drains to the blinking red zone. The toothless vagrant with the bird nest beard and tattered jeans runs from his tent to help me up.

"Are you the monster slayer?" he says, and I nod. Yes, I am the monster slayer.

The vagrant unfolds a soiled piece of paper covered in some kind of hobo hieroglyphics and says it's a map. I can't make sense of the symbols, but I read them as if I understand, and when I look up, the vagrant is gone and where he'd been standing is a floating black oblong, a portal. I can hear Kira's voice and Emery's laughter coming from inside of the portal and I dive inside.

Loading. . . loading. . . loading. . .

fireworks

It's New Year's Eve and we want to give baby girl a fireworks show so we drive out to Asa's. No burn ban out in the sticks. We stop at a fireworks stand along the way and the old redneck working it says he's got the real shit under this tarp around back, if we're interested. The fun stuff.

"That's what we want," Kira says. "The fun stuff."

We come away with a backseat full of colorful explosives. Emery pulls a sky rocket from one of the boxes and taps the rocket against the window, mouth and eyes wide in wonder. From where she sits, the rocket seems to be flying across the sky.

We line up the rockets in the scalped-to-dirt yard and aim away from the trees as best as we can. We blow up the sky with red and white dahlias. Chrysanthemum bursts of green, purple, blue.

Emery bounces on Kira's shoulders, gasping and pointing and pulling at her momma's hair.

Kira is near throwed off Ramuné lean, an offering of Asa's—"Champagne for my real friends," as he puts it. I ask for a sip and Kira shakes her head. Smiles. I say, "Just a taste." She grabs my shirt and puts her tongue in my mouth. That grape syrup medicinal candy taste. Emery kicks me in the face.

It's a small gathering. Raymond, Isaac, Percy, Briana and her girlfriend, and this big chick who hangs around Asa.

We blow through the fireworks. Pork chops, greens, and black-eyed peas on paper plates. Emery rides around on Donatello the tortoise's back.

Empty bottles of that Japanese soda—glasses streaked purple with codeine residue—are scattered about among the smoking, blown-apart rocket tubes on the ground.

Young Thug's "Digits" on a Bluetooth speaker.

"Why not risk life when it's gon' keep going?"

The women dance in the brightness of a floodlight. Kira with her hands in the air, pendulum-swinging her hips.

Emery rubs her eyes and yawns. I scoop her off the tortoise and she lays her head on my shoulder.

"When you die, somebody else is born."

Raymond says, "You got yourself a real one," nodding at Kira.

"She rolls with the punches," I say. "Keeps me grounded. I'd fall to pieces without her."

"Two girls who love you to death." Raymond rustles Emery's hair, says, "You winning, my nigga."

"At least we got to say. . . we ran up them digits, we ran up the money."

Isaac finds an intact rocket that had toppled over. Lights it while holding the stick. Kira spins in slow circles, eyes closed, feeling the beat. Vibing. The rocket explodes in a crown of fiery glitter above her head.

Sins of the Father

Kira's dad is locked up in Clemens for trying to rob the dollar store after popping an Ambien. It'd have probably been chalked up as what it was, a side effect of a bad drug, if he hadn't been buck-ass naked waving around a hunting rifle. Today's his birthday, so the three of us are on our way to visit him. Nice little family trip to prison.

Kira and I are going back and forth on who we might have been in past lives. "Bonnie and Clyde," she says, "obviously. But who else?"

I ask if she thinks we've known each other in every lifetime and she says, "Only the good ones."

Miles of farmland and cell towers.

Spotify shuffles UGK, Deftones, Nina Simone, Bush.

Kira is turned around in the shotgun seat, trying to get Emery to sing the happy birthday song. She makes faces and claps her hands. She sings, "Happy birthday. . . to you."

Emery kicks her feet and cackles at the ceiling. She says, "No!"

We each grab one of Emery's hands and one two three swing her through the metal detector.

Kira signs us in. The guard asks if we'd like a coloring page for the little one. He holds up a box of crayons and a black-and-white page of prison-themed illustrations: a smiling guard in the sniper tower, a wide-eyed inmate in cuffs, a straight razor, a riot baton.

I shake my head. Kira says, "Yeah, nah, we're good."

We take our seats in the waiting room. A woman in a black sequin top and leopard print leggings sits crying mascara streaks across from us.

Emery stares. "Ah wu otay?" she says.

The woman responds by crying harder, palms pressed over her eyes.

Kira bounces her leg, picks the skin around her thumbnail. I reach over and grab her hand.

"He said he didn't want to see her, last I talked to him on the phone," she says.

I remember the conversation, or at least the side of it I heard from outside the house.

"He said this is no place to bring a child. But what, does he want to meet his granddaughter when she's a teenager? Who is he to tell us where to take our kid?"

A guard steps into the room, names the inmates next in line to talk on phones behind glass. Through the open door, we can see Kira's dad standing there, bouncing on his heels. He's skin and bones. He rubs his palms, shoulders slumped. I hold Emery up and wave her arm for her. Kira says, "Say hi to Grandpa," and that's when he notices. And that's when his mouth drops but we never hear the words that come out. That's when his eyes swell up puffy and red and he tries to shove the inmate behind him out of the way but he's too frail and so he presses himself against the wall and shimmies back to the cell block, and that's when Kira shouts at him over the guard's shoulder, "Fuck you! You selfish fucking bastard!"

Emery joins in the shouting. Kicks her feet and throws both hands in the air. Says, "Hap birfday!"

A THOUSAND
MORE
LIFETIMES

A haze of drywall dust fills the cab of Percy's truck. The scratching only makes the fiberglass dig deeper into my pores, but I can't help going at it until my arms are glowing red. Percy grabs each of us a tall boy from the cooler behind the seat and he cracks his while steering with his knee and I roll the can between my forearms. That soothing coldness. Percy crushes the empty and hooks it out the window into the truck bed.

He's hyped about whatever it is he's going on about, way he keeps smacking my shoulder, but everything he says is coming from somewhere deep underwater. The Kalm high is wearing off. Sharp polygons soften and the afternoon sun pierces through the grungy darkness. The volume cranks up slow and warbled.

"—got that roast beef pussy, know what I mean? Now I can't look at a sandwich without my stomach getting all knotted up."

I don't know what to add to that, so I say, "Damn, that's crazy," and the rest of the ride to my place is mostly spent in silence.

My arms have stopped itching.

I crack the beer.

Way Kira tells it, she spent a solid five repeats of "All That I've Got" trying to hype herself up in the car. She's still wearing the ski mask, still holding the gun. The bed is blanketed in dollar bills of all denominations. Kira says it was the old man working the register when she upped the PLR at the glass. I picture her upping it with both hands, the way she's doing now, acting it all out again—so the old man and me, we're both staring down the barrel of this .40 caliber hand cannon—chipped pink fingernails and rigid black steel—and Kira says the old man's faith in the glass must have been weak because he pops the drawer without argument, shoulders slumped, hands shaking—she's screaming at him just like she's screaming at me now to hurry the fuck up, to empty the drawer in one of those plastic bags with the smiley face and shove it under the glass—THANK YOU COME AGAIN—The Used as soundtrack to armed robbery—*"I'll be just fine pretending I'm not."*

There's something intrinsically familiar about all of this. In every incarnation, I know she's been my ride-or-die.

I ask where Emery is while this is going down, while Kira's running with the bag full of money to where she parked inside the car wash, outside of camera range. Kira says she's fine, she left her with my mom. And now she's unbuckling my belt and licking the dust off my neck.

She shakes her hips as I peel off her jeans. We spread the bills around the bed with all the movement.

She's still wearing the ski mask, still holding the gun, but now all of her clothes are on the floor and she bites my ear, twists the barrel under my chin. She says, "Tell me you want me," and she doesn't have to say it twice.

The back of her head smacks the wall. She grits her teeth and pulls my hair. Her legs spasm wrapped around my waist and she bucks and says *oh, god* and I thrust deeper and come inside her and we collapse together, tangled in each other's limbs, her hands draped over my shoulders. The cold steel of the gun against my back.

We lie like this for a thousand more lifetimes, knowing that two in the morning will mean a screaming child cutting another tooth, and we'll be gathered in front of the glow of some late-night anime all zoned out and blinking along in the syncopated rhythm of Emery banging on a toy drum. Leaned up against the trash I forgot to take out will sit the last attempt at the canvas before it's tossed. "That feeling I was trying to express,"

Kira will say, "I figured it out," and then she'll dip her finger in the wet hot pink acrylic of a forever unfinished painting and she'll draw a cross on my temple and say she's going to help me let out the devils, and she'll squeeze the trigger of a power drill slow at first, revving up as the bit spins closer to my head, and I won't be sure if she's joking or not, but I'm not going to stop her.

Kelby Losack is a woodworking artisan and carpenter by trade. His other books are *Hurricane Season*, *Dead Boy* (with J. David Osborne), *The Way We Came In*, and *Heathenish*. He is the co-host of *Agitator*, an extreme Japanese cinema podcast. He lives with his wife in Gulf Coast Texas.

Twitter: @HeathenishKid
Instagram: @kelby.losack

ACKNOWLEDGMENTS

Not enough thanks can be given.

To Erika, for being a true ride-or-die and always thugging it out with me. I love you, babe, for a thousand more lifetimes.

To JDO, my brother.

To Kazepis for making the shit look good, and for all the hours just chopping it up.

To Lucas and Grant for the daily motivation.

Of course shouts out to the homie Marcus.

To my hometown heroes Lunv D, Infennity, Derrick Peoples, and That Mexican OT.

To Mom and Dad.

To the kids.

To *Apocalypse Confidential* for running an excerpt of this, and just for existing.

To Braden, Sierra, Cody, Rios de la Luz, Brian Allen Carr, Jeremy Robert Johnson, Jordan Harper, D'urban Moffer, John Wayne Comunale, Max Booth III, Tom Wickersham, Matt Neil Hill, Scott Adlerberg, Michael J. Seidlinger, Chris Kelso, Josh Jabcuga, David Simmons, Cory Bennet, Troy James Weaver,

Jack, Ortant, Brendan, Barrett Avner, Luis Galindo, Sam Pink, Sean Kilpatrick, Lil Durt, Hextape, Benoit Lelievre, Ben over at *Neon Pajamas*, Max Thrax, Blauer, Daniel Feldman, Tobias Carroll, Diamond Kennedy, Andrew Hilbert, Eddie and the Car Crash boys, Zach Langley Chi-Chi, Keenan Maxie, David James Keaton, Jedidiah Ayres, Baby Trill, Gordon White, Joe D, Cloud, Lord Bile, Worstnightmare, Jeff Weiss, Jose, Kane, Kevin, Justin Carter, Bud Smith, Chris Campanioni, Francois Pointeau, Robert Dean, Cody Goodfellow, Stephen Graham Jones, Anthony Trevino, Eddie Rathke, Elle Nash, Brian Alan Ellis, Matthew Revert, Cavin Gonzalez, *LitReactor*, and everyone still fucking with me. The messages, phone calls, shouts out, platforms, the inspiration. . . I think you're all great.

Music I listened to while writing this: LXST CXNTURY, Lorn, Filmmaker, Salem, The Body, Uniform, Getter, Shlohmo, Earl Sweatshirt, 070 Shake, 03 Greedo, Drakeo the Ruler, Kent Loon, Chester Watson, Danny Brown, The Dillinger Escape Plan, Tchami, Charli XCX, Ludovico Einaudi, UGK, Young Thug, Z-Ro, Trippjones, Wargasm, Tyler the Creator, Bones, Schemaposse, AshTreJinkins, Dusty Locane, Sheff G, Chat Pile, Dos Monos, Lil Wayne, Tomahawk, RXK Nephew, RX Papi, Axxturel, Slurr, 2Shanes, Baddcitizen, Xxxtentacion, Have a Nice Life, Electric Wizard, KFC Murder Chicks, 42 Dugg, 24kGoldn, OmenXIII, Aj Suede, IC3PEAK, ndls404, boneles_s, White Ring, and a few others probably, but. . .

Made in the USA
Coppell, TX
24 June 2022

79179124R00076